Beauty and the Beast

Illustrated by
CHARLES MOORE
with assistance from Tami Hodge

RIZZOLI
NEW YORK

To Mimi Weingarten

First published in the United States of America in 1991 by
Rizzoli International Publications, Inc.
300 Park Avenue South, New York, New York 10010

Illustration copyright © 1991 Charles Moore
Text and compilation copyright © 1991
Rizzoli International Publications, Inc.

Library of Congress Cataloging-in-Publication Data

Perrault, Charles, 1628–1703.
    Beauty and the beast/retold by Charles Perrault;
illustrated by Charles Moore.
        p.   cm.
    Summary: Through her great capacity to love, a kind
and beautiful maid releases a handsome prince from the
spell which has made him an ugly beast.
    ISBN 0-8478-1368-1
    [1. Fairy tales. 2. Folklore—France.]   I. Moore,
Charles Willard, 1925–   ill.   II. Title.
PZ8.P426Be   1991   90-26307
398.21′0944—dc20   CIP
                                  AC

Typography by Graphic Arts Composition
Printed and bound by Tien Wah Press, Singapore

Design by Milton Glaser, Inc.

Beauty and the Beast

ONCE UPON A TIME, there lived a rich merchant, a widower, who had three daughters. The youngest was admired by everyone. When she was small she was known simply as "the little beauty," and this name stuck to her, causing a great deal of jealousy among her sisters.

This youngest girl was not only prettier than her sisters, but very much nicer. The two elder girls were very arrogant and pretended to be great ladies, refusing to visit with the daughters of other merchants, and associating only with nobility.

Now these girls were known to be very rich and, as a result, were sought in marriage by many prominent merchants. The two eldest said they would never marry unless they could find a duke, or at least a count. Beauty, however, very politely thanked all who proposed marriage to her, but said that she was too young at present, and that she wished to keep her father company for several years yet.

Suddenly, the merchant lost his fortune. The only property which remained to him was a house in the country, a long way from the city. With tears he broke the news to his children, telling them that they would have to move to this house and work very hard to help make ends meet.

WHEN they had settled in the country, Beauty would rise with the sun, and kept busy all day looking after the house and preparing dinner for the family. In her leisure time, she read, or played the harpsichord, or sang at her spinning wheel.

Her two sisters, on the other hand, were very lazy; they did not get up until noon, and they idled about all day. Their only diversion was to bemoan the beautiful clothes they had once worn and the company they used to keep. "Look at our little sister," they would say to each other, "her tastes are so low and her mind so slow that she is quite content with this miserable state of affairs."

The merchant, however, was greatly impressed by Beauty's good qualities and especially by her patience—for her sisters not only left her all the work of the house, but never missed an opportunity to insult her.

One day the merchant received a letter informing him that a ship on which he had some merchandise had just come safely to port. The two elder girls were overjoyed for they thought that at last they would be able to quit their dull life in the country. When they saw their father ready to set out they begged him to bring them back dresses, jewelry, and finery of every kind. Beauty asked for nothing, thinking that all the money which the merchandise might yield would not be enough to satisfy her sisters' greedy demands.

"You have asked for nothing," said her father. "As you are so kind to think of me," she replied, "please bring me a rose for there are none here."

WHEN the merchant reached port, he sold the contents of the ship. However, after settling his debts, he discovered there was no money left for the fine things his daughters had desired—not even a single rose for Beauty.

Upon his return trip home, he had to pass through a large wood. It was storming horribly, and he could no longer see the path.

Suddenly, he saw a strong light at the end of a long avenue of trees. He rode towards it and presently discovered that it came from an immense palace that was magnificently lit up.

THE MERCHANT hastened to the palace. To his surprise, he found no one about in the courtyards nor did anyone answer his cries of "hello" when he entered the great hall. In the banquet room, he discovered a good fire, and a table laden with food, but with a place set for only one.

He waited a considerable time, but still did not see or hear anyone. No longer able to resist his hunger, he sat down at the table and ate heartily, not leaving a single crumb. "I am sure," he remarked to himself, "that the master of this house or his servants will forgive the liberty I am taking; doubtless, they will be here soon." Becoming bolder, he ventured out of the room and passed through several lavishly furnished apartments. Finding a room with a bed, he decided to retire as he was exhausted.

When he rose the next morning, he returned to the room where he had supped the night before, and found there a table laid for breakfast. "This place," he thought, "must surely belong to some good fairy, who has taken pity on my plight."

Having eaten his fill, the good man went outdoors to seek the path that led homewards. As he passed under a bower of roses he remembered that Beauty had asked for one, and plucked a spray from a mass of blooms.

THE VERY SAME MOMENT, he heard a terrible noise, and saw a beast coming towards him which was so hideous that he could not bear to look at it.

"Ungrateful wretch!" said the Beast, in a dreadful voice. "I have saved your life by receiving you into my home from the storm, and in return you steal that which I love more than anything in the world—my roses. You shall pay for this with your life!"

The merchant fell to his knees and began wringing his hands. "Pardon, my lord," he cried. "One of my daughters had asked for a rose, and I did not dream I would be giving offense by picking one."

"I am not called 'my lord,'" answered the monster, "but 'The Beast.' Do not hope to soften me with such flattery. You have daughters, you say; well, I am willing to pardon you if one of your daughters will come, of her own choice, to die in your place. Do not argue with me—go! And swear that if your daughters refuse to come in your place, you will come back again within three months."

The good man had no intention of sacrificing one of his daughters to this hideous monster, but he thought that at least he might have the pleasure of seeing them once more. He therefore swore to return, and the Beast said, "You shall not go home empty-handed. Upon your arrival, you will find a chest, the contents of which shall benefit your family." With these words, the Beast withdrew.

The merchant set forth from the palace, as distraught now as he had been joyous when he entered it.

SOON he was home. His daughters crowded around him, but at the sight of them, he burst into tears. In his hand was the bunch of roses which he had brought for Beauty. He gave it to her saying: "Take these roses, Beauty; it is dearly that your poor father will have to pay for them."

Thereupon, he told his daughters of the dire adventure that had befallen him. On hearing the tale the two elder girls began to cry and scolded Beauty for not weeping.

"It would be quite useless to weep," said Beauty. "Why should I lament my father's death? He is not going to die. Since the monster agrees to accept a daughter instead, I intend to offer myself to appease his fury."

"I am touched by the goodness of Beauty's heart and intention, but I will not expose her to death," replied the merchant. "I am old and have not much longer to live; and I shall merely lose a few years that will be regretted only on account of you, my dear children."

"I assure you, Father," said Beauty, "that you will not go to this place without me. You cannot prevent me from following you. I would rather be devoured by this monster than die of grief which your loss would cause me." Words were useless. Beauty was quite determined to go to the palace, and her sisters were not sorry.

The merchant was so taken with the sorrow of losing his daughter that he had forgotten all about the Beast's promise. To his astonishment, when he had retired to his room for the night, the chest was at the side of his bed! Inside was gold enough to restore the family to their original place in society.

SOON Beauty set off with her father. By evening they saw the palace, all lit up as before. When the good merchant and his daughter entered the banquet room, they saw a table magnificently laid for two people. The merchant had not the heart to eat, but Beauty, forcing herself to appear calm, sat down and served him.

When they had finished supper, they heard a terrible noise. With tears the merchant bade farewell to his daughter, for he knew it was the Beast. Beauty herself could not help trembling when she saw the creature, but she did her best to smile and remain calm. The Beast asked her if she had come of her own free will, and she timidly answered that such was the case.

"You are indeed kind," said the Beast, "and I am much obliged to you. You, my good man, will depart tomorrow morning, and you must not think of coming back again." Upon saying this, the monster disappeared.

"Daughter," said the merchant, embracing Beauty, "I am nearly dead with fright for you. Let me be the one to stay here!"

"No, father," said Beauty, firmly. "Perhaps pity will be taken on me."

They retired for the evening, thinking they would not sleep at all during the night, but they were hardly in bed before their eyes were closed in sleep.

*T*HE NEXT MORNING after the merchant departed, Beauty sat down in the great hall and began to cry. But she soon stopped as she had plenty of courage, and she determined to grieve no more during the short time she had yet to live, as she was convinced that the Beast would devour her that night. She began a tour of the beautiful building and its gardens, the splendor of which she could not but admire.

*I*MAGINE her surprise when she came
upon a door on which were the words
"Beauty's Room"! She quickly opened this
door, and was dazzled by the magnificence of
the furnishings within.

"The Beast is evidently anxious that
I should not be bored," she murmured,
as she caught sight of a large bookcase, a
harpsichord, and several volumes of music. A
moment later another thought crossed her
mind. "If I had only a day to spend here," she
reflected, "such thoughtful attention would
surely not have been paid to me."

This notion gave her fresh courage. She
approached the bookcase, and found a book
in which was written, in letters of gold:

> Ask for anything you wish;
> you are mistress of all here.

Beauty could not but think that the Beast
was very kind, and that she had nothing
much to fear from him.

IN THE EVENING, as she was about to sit down at the table, she heard the noise made by the Beast, and quaked in spite of herself.

"Beauty," said the monster, "may I watch you have your supper?"

"You are master here," said the trembling Beauty.

"Not so," replied the Beast. "It is you who are mistress; you have only to tell me to go, if my presence annoys you, and I will go immediately. Tell me, now, do you consider me very ugly?"

"I do," said Beauty, "since I must speak the truth; but I think you are also very kind."

"It is as you say," said the monster, "and in addition to being ugly, I lack intelligence. As I am aware, I am a mere beast."

"It is not the way with stupid people," answered Beauty, "to admit a lack of intelligence. Fools never realize it."

"Sup well, Beauty," said the monster, "and try to banish dullness from your new home—for all about you is yours, and I should be sorry to think you were not happy."

"You are indeed kind," said Beauty. "With one thing I am well pleased, and that is your kind heart. When I think of that, you no longer seem to be ugly. There are many handsome men who make worse monsters than you. I prefer you, notwithstanding your looks, to those who under pretty smiles hide false, corrupt, and ungrateful hearts."

"Then, Beauty, will you be my wife?" asked the Beast.

For some time, she did not answer, fearing lest she might anger the monster by her refusal. She summoned up courage at last to say, rather fearfully, "No, Beast."

The poor monster gave forth so terrible a sigh that the noise of it echoed through the whole palace. He sadly took his leave of Beauty. Alone, Beauty was moved by great compassion for this poor Beast.

"What a pity he is so ugly," she said, "for he is so good."

BEAUTY passed three months in the palace quite happily. Every evening the Beast paid her a visit, and entertained her at supper. And every day Beauty was made aware of some fresh kindness on the part of the monster. Through seeing him often she had become accustomed to his ugliness, and far from dreading the moment of his visit, she anticipated it with much impatience.

One thing alone troubled Beauty: every evening, before retiring to bed, the monster asked her if she would be his wife, and he seemed overwhelmed with grief when she refused.

"You distress me, Beast," she finally confided. "I wish I could marry you, but I can not deceive you by allowing you to believe this could ever be. I will always be your friend—please be content with that."

"I suppose I must," replied the Beast. "But let me make the situation clear. I know I am very terrible, but I love you very much, and I shall be very happy if you will only remain here. Promise that you will never leave me."

Beauty blushed at these words. "I would willingly promise to remain with you always," she said to the Beast, "but I have so great a desire to see my father again that I feel I shall die of grief if you refuse me this favor. I promise I shall return to you in one week."

"You shall be with him tomorrow morning," said the Beast. "But remember your promise. If you fail to return by the seventh day, then I will surely die from loneliness. On the seventh day all you have to do when you wish to return is to put your ring on a table when you are going to bed. Good-bye, Beauty!"

SHE AWOKE the next morning to find herself in her old bedroom in her father's house. She rang a little bell by her bed, and it was answered by their servant, who gave a great cry at the sight of her. The good merchant came running at the noise, and was overwhelmed with joy at the sight of his dear daughter.

Her sisters were mortified when they saw Beauty dressed like a princess from the wardrobe the Beast had provided her. Her caresses were ignored, and the jealously which they could not stifle only grew worse when she told them how happy she was. Out into the garden went the envious pair.

"Why should our *dear* sister be happier than we are?" each demanded of the other.

"I have an idea," said one. "Let us persuade her to stay here longer than the seven days. Her stupid Beast will fly into a rage when he finds she has broken her word, and will very likely devour her."

"You are right, sister," replied the other. "But we must make a great fuss over her if we are to make the plan successful."

With this plot decided upon they went indoors again, and paid such attention to their little sister that Beauty wept for joy. When the seven days had passed the two elder sisters cried so forlornly that she promised to remain another week.

BEAUTY reproached herself, nevertheless, for the grief she was causing the poor Beast; moreover, she greatly missed seeing him. On the tenth night of her stay in her father's house, she dreamed that she was in the palace garden, where she saw the Beast lying on the grass as if dead. Beauty woke with a start.

"I am indeed wicked," she said, "to cause so much grief to a Beast who has shown me nothing but kindness. Is it his fault that he is so ugly and has few wits? He is good, and that makes up for all the rest. Why did I not wish to marry him? It is neither good looks nor brains in one's mate that makes one happy; it is beauty of character, virtue, and kindness. All these qualities the Beast has. He has my esteem, friendship, and gratitude. At all events, I must not make him miserable, or I shall reproach myself all my life."

With these words, Beauty placed her ring on her side table and fell back asleep.

When she awoke the next morning she saw with joy that she was in the Beast's palace. She dressed hurriedly and then ran from room to room calling the Beast by name: but in vain, for he did not appear. Recalling her dream, she dashed into the garden by the fountain, where she had seen him in her sleep. There she found the poor Beast lying unconscious, and she thought he must be dead. She threw herself on his body, all horror of his looks forgotten, and feeling his heart still beating, she fetched water from the fountain and threw it on his face.

THE BEAST opened his eyes and said, "You forgot your promise. The grief I felt at having lost you made me resolve to die, but I do so content since I have the pleasure of seeing you once more."

"Forgive me, dear Beast," said Beauty, "and do not die, but live and become my husband. Here and now I offer you my hand, and swear that I will marry none but you. Alas, I fancied I felt only friendship for you, but the sorrow I have experienced clearly proves to me that I cannot live without you."

Beauty had scarce uttered these words when the palace became ablaze with lights and fireworks filled the air. But these splendors were lost on her; she turned to her dear Beast, still trembling for his danger.

To her surprise, the Beast had disappeared. In his place, stood a beautiful prince who bowed to her.

"But where is my Beast?" asked the bewildered Beauty.

"You see him before you," answered the Prince. "A wicked fairy placed me under a spell to appear as the Beast until a beautiful girl should consent to marry me of her own free will. You alone in all the world showed yourself susceptible to the kindness of my character. Although no longer the Beast, if you believe you may learn to love me in this form, then I offer both myself and my crown to you in thanks and devotion for what you have done."

Beauty married the Prince and they lived together for a long time in happiness.

CHARLES W. MOORE, *a Fellow of the American Institute of Architects, has been an internationally acclaimed architect for well over two decades. His work, writing, and teaching have profoundly influenced the course of American architecture since his early award-winning work at The Sea Ranch in Northern California in 1964. Moore is the 1991 recipient of the American Institute of Architects' prestigious Gold Medal as well as more than 25 national awards for architectural design, including national AIA Honor Awards in both 1987 and 1988.*

Committed to education as well as practice, he has taught nearly continuously for the last forty years, from Princeton and Yale (where he was dean) to the University of California at Berkeley (where he was chairman for three years) and the University of California at Los Angeles. Since 1984, he has held the O'Neil Ford Centennial Chair in Architecture at the University of Texas at Austin and is the recent winner of the Topaz Medallion for Excellency in Architectural Education.

Moore's built work ranges from houses and housing to world's fairs, art institutions, civic centers, and university campuses. His work in campus planning and public institutions includes Kresge College, the University of California at Santa Cruz, the Hood Museum at Dartmouth College, and the Beverly Hills Civic Center. Throughout his work, Moore has retained a deep appreciation for the uniqueness of the places where he is asked to build. He fuses this sense of place with an enthusiasm for participatory design and a noted sensitivity to the dreams and aspirations of his clients.